Mommy I Want 2 Fly

AuthorHouse™
1663 Liberty Drive
Bloomington, IN 47403
www.authorhouse.com
Phone: 833-262-8899

This book is printed on acid-free paper.

ISBN: 978-1-7283-6636-4 (sc)
978-1-7283-6638-8 (hc)
978-1-7283-6637-1 (e)

Library of Congress Control Number: 2021904810

Print information available on the last page.

Published by AuthorHouse 07/28/2020

authorHOUSE®

Authors Inspiration

Someone asked me, what motivated me to write children's books? I could only come up with two reasons: first and foremost the children, last and not least my unfortunate circumstances. You see when a judge sentence you to thirty years and you have to do fifteen of them, then you are put into a cell no bigger than the average bathroom, you do two things: first you hunger for your departure, craving your freedom, second you wonder what it is, or what happen for you to be in this situation. I could not help but to reflect back, and trace the steps of my life to this point. What I realized was that it was my environment. Most people say that they were in the wrong place at the wrong time. I personally feel I grew up in the wrong place at the wrong time. In this environment, there were only two things you could do, die trying to get out or live trying to survive the environment.

The role model was obsolete for me. I had no father figure to show me how to become a man. The men that were in my life had no morals. Their lives were dedicated to one thing, investing their way of life on children, to give them a means of finance, without being in the forefront. Like anyone with a desire to have more than they already have, I fell victim to that lifestyle. So, I started asking myself whose fault is this? What would I do if I found out whose fault it really was? Inside, I formed a pain, a hate, and I felt as if vengeance was mine. It was too late to stop what had already had happened in my life.

So I wondered, and asked myself, how can I help the innocent children who are having their rights of innocence stripped away from them? The only thing I could think of was what would hold a child's undivided attention? What would be there for a child when he/she had nothing else? Three things came to mind: laughter, love, and an imagination. With those thoughts in mind, I began to write books for children. I felt that not only would the books hold their attention, but it will cause them to laugh, as well as imagine. I was once told that energy never disappears, but transforms from one form to another. So today I dedicate all of my energy to the greatest vision a man could ever have that is in our children. This vision will keep them safe and innocent. That's why I write books for children. In closing I would like to thank our heavenly father.

BY: VERNON T. BATEMAN

ACKNOWLEDGEMENTS

I would like to begin by giving honor to God, for giving me the inspiration and knowledge to write this book. It started off as a gift to my beautiful daughter, *Heaven Bateman* a. k. a. my little butterfly. After further conversations with her she wanted me to share this powerful message with other children around the world.

I would like to Especially Thank my mother Donna Franklyn for always believing in me and not giving up on me. I also want to thank and acknowledge the mother of my daughter; "Shameka Kirksey"; You may Forever Rest in Peace. I want to give a Special Thank You, to the Wonderful Ms. Minnie

As always, thanks to my Support team, Board members, and all that donated their time, effort and skills during my founding and the operation of **"Kids with a Cause.us";** non-profit organization. Nelreca, Nora, Crystal, Donnell, Ollie Anne, Nicole, La Paul, Promise, Mishawn, Angel, Saquan, Miracle, Grandma Dorothy, Darian, Mrs. Thurman, Mrs. Smith, Chris "LA" Jackson, Nate, and Big Cal. Thanks to my good friend Eric "E" Kuykendall for help with typing and editing.

An extra special thanks to Congressman Andre' Carson, Brittany Taylor, and his staff for their support and encouragement, most importantly, for giving me the opportunity to continue succeeding.

There are so many people that make you successful; I could not list them all. Please know that I thank you very much for your faith in me, you're countless prayers, and motivating words.

For this I will always be grateful.

Vernon T. Bateman

Mommy I Want To Fly

AUTHOR AND ILLUSTRATOR

VERNON T. BATEMAN

CHILDRENS BOOK

LITERARY WORK

Poppa Unity� Momma Lovely� Sister Loyalty
Butterfly   Butterfly   Butterfly� Little

Modesty

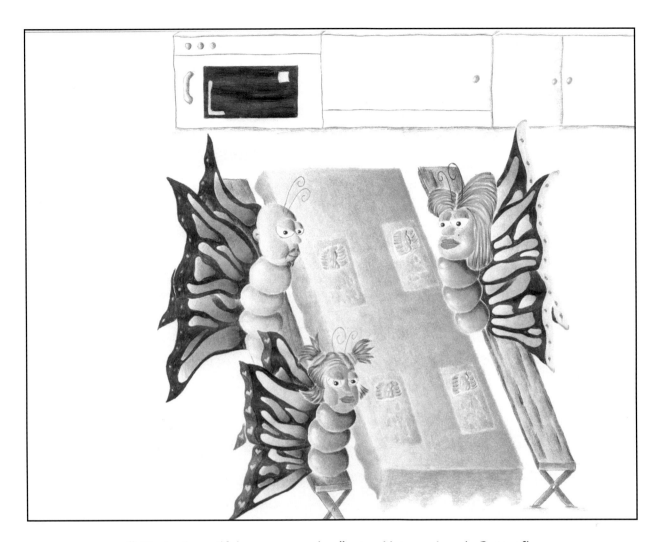

"What a beautiful sunny morning," says Mommy Lovely Butterfly,
as she prepares breakfast for her family.

Papa Unity Butterfly notices an empty chair at the table. He asks his
daughter Loyalty, "Where is your brother, Lil Modesty?"

"He's still in bed. He is kind of sad," said Loyalty.

"Why?" asked Papa, "Pancakes and fresh sun flower seeds are his favorite breakfast."

"I know Papa, it's not the breakfast. It is the beautiful weather," said
Loyalty. "Modesty hasn't developed his wings yet."

"Oh dear," says Mama Lovely, "I need to fly up and check on him."

When Momma Lovely reached her son's room, she noticed a sign on the door. The sign read, "Do Not Disturb."

Momma Lovely knocked on the door. *Knock, knock, knock, knock.*

"Come in," said Lil Modesty in a small whining voice.

Momma Lovely entered the room, and notice Lil Modesty still in bed, with a sad expression on his face.

"Hey baby, what's wrong?" asked Momma Lovely. "I made your favorite breakfast, pancakes and sunflower seeds."

In the same whining voice, Lil Modesty replied, "I know, I can smell it.
Mommy, when will I grow beautiful wings?" Lil Modesty asked.

"I want so badly to enjoy the nice weather, and feel the warm sun, or feel the
breeze through my wings. Birds have wings, and bees, and flies, have them. Even
fleas!" he explained. "It's not fair! It's just not fair!" Lil Modesty pouted.

When Momma Lovely opened her mouth to responded, Lil Modesty said
in a sad, dismal voice, "Mommy, will I ever get my wings?"

"Oh baby," said Momma Lovely, "butterfly wings are different than any other wings on earth. Unlike other creatures, butterflies do not get their wings right away. That's why they are so beautiful."

"I don't understand, mommy," said Lil Modesty with a confused look. "Why do my wings have to take so long?"

"Our wings are earned," said Momma Lovely. "They are developed by our character and behavior."

"Well Mommy, I've been good. Can you give me my wings? Please, please, please...." begged Lil Modesty".

Momma Lovely said, "I cannot give you wings, but I can prepare you. I can teach you, but more importantly, I can nurture you and you will grow and develop strong, beautiful wings."

"Really? Really, Mommy?" Lil Modesty exclaimed.

"That's right Modesty," said Momma Lovely. "But first, let's start with nurturing your tummy. Come down and eat your breakfast with the family."

"Okay Mommy, thanks" Modesty said happily.

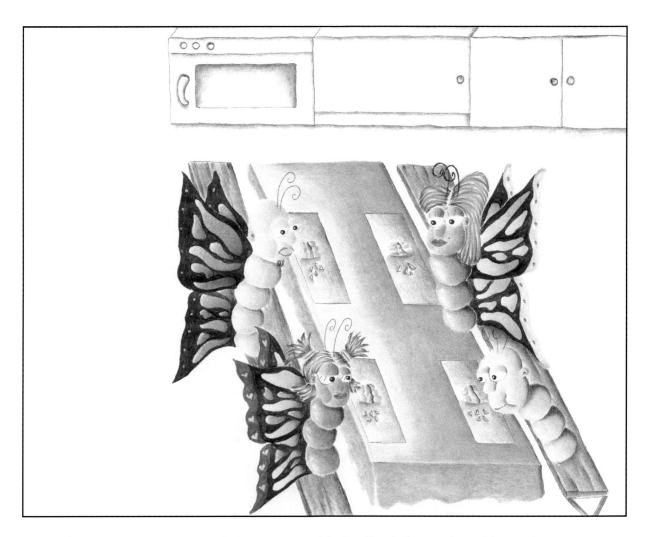

Lil Modesty entered the kitchen and saw his family sitting at the table ready to eat.

Papa Unity saw his son and said happily, "Hey, there, top of the morning to you son. You're just in time to say grace."

After grace was said, Papa asked Lil Modesty, "How are you this morning?"

"I'm fine Papa, but I am still a little confused, replied Modesty. "Anything I can help you with son?" Papa asked.

"Well, Mommy said I have to earn my wings, but I'm not sure how," said Modesty. "Oh son that's easy," said Papa, "just live up to your name."

"Am I too young to be modest?" Modesty asked. "Will I still be able to have fun and play?"

"Sure you will son," said Papa. "It's fun to be modest. Look at it as a gift! The trick to this gift is... in order to keep it, you have to give it away. A gift so beautiful it is meant to be shared. Morals and principles have their own rules. The more you share them, the more you will receive them."

"Wow," said Modesty. "I think I got it, Pops!"

Sister Loyalty said, "I never looked at it like that. Do you mean, the more loyal I am to someone, the more someone will be loyal to me?"

"Yep for the most part, that's true" said Papa.

"The more respect and love I share," said Momma, "the more love and respect is shared with me."

"I have an idea," said Loyalty. "There's a big checker tournament at the Summer Fair this weekend. You can practice on being modest at the fair. Everyone will be there, even Lisa the Lady Bug," teased Loyalty.

"Who is Lisa the Lady Bug?" Mommy asked curiously.

"Modesty's sweetheart," Loyalty said laughing. "He tries to impress her, but he's too shy because he does not have any wings. That's why he never talks to her."

"Oh, that's cute," said Momma.

"Aww Mommy," said Modesty sheepishly.

Papa cut in and said, "Don't worry son, I have a close friend who happens to be the best checker player in the entire forest.

His name is Bubble Gum Bunny. He can prepare you for the tournament. He should be at the park, but if you go, remember not to go to the park by yourself."

"That's right," Momma agreed. "After you finish your breakfast, you can ask some of your friends if they would like to go to the park. And stay away from the Peppermint Snake Stranger."

"Yummy, I love peppermints," said Modesty.

"No, no, no Modesty, "Momma exclaimed. "Those peppermints smell and look good, but they come from strangers. The Peppermint Snake Stranger's peppermints are bad and will hurt you."

"Okay Mama. I'll stay away from them," Modesty promised.

"Do you remember the password?" asked Papa. "Yes, I remember," said Modesty.

Okay. Mama asked, " If a stranger, no matter who they are or what they say, even if they say me or your fathers name and want you to go with them, what do you say?'

"What's the password," replied Modesty. "Right!" said Momma.

"That's right," said Papa proudly, "And what is the password, Modesty and Loyalty?

Lil Modesty replied with enthusiasm, "Mashed Potatoes!"

"And the password is a family secret," Papa said with a smile.

After breakfast, Lil Modesty headed out to find his friends at their favorite hangout, The Big Mushroom. When it's hot, and the sun is shining bright, they love The Big Mushroom for its cool shade.

As Lil Modesty approached The Big Mushroom, a big smile was on his face. He noticed three of his best friends were under The Big Mushroom, Sniggles the Snail, Whispers the Turtle, and Ding Dong the Dragonfly.

"Hey guys," Modesty shouts. "Hi Modesty," they all say at once.

"You guys want to go to the park with me today ?"

"Sure," said Sniggles, "we will go to the park with you."

"I like the park," said Ding Dong. "I always have fun there."

"There is a big checker tournament this weekend, and I'm going to sign up. Maybe it will help me earn my wings!" said Modesty with excitement.

"How will a checker tournament help you with earning your wings?" asked Whispers.

"I'm not sure, but I have a good feeling it will," replied Modesty.

"That sounds great!" said Whispers, "But why are we going to the park?"

"Papa says that Bubble Gum Bunny is the best checker player in the entire forest," said Modesty, "and he will be at the park today. I'm hoping he will help me prepare for the checker tournament."

"Sounds exciting!" said Ding Dong, "Let's go guys!"

Whispers the Turtle also heard amazing stories about Bubble Gum Bunny. He even beat ten guys at the same time. They all headed to the park, as Whispers shared more stories.

Ding Dong became so excited, that he flew far ahead while leading the pack and we could barely see him.

"Hey, slow down!" Modesty yelled. "We have to be careful and stay together."

"Why?" Sniggles asked, "He knows the way to the park."

"Yeah," Whispers agreed. "He won't get lost."

"It's not that he will get lost," replied Modesty. "It's just that I promised my parents we would all stay together and be careful, because of the Peppermint Snake Strangers."

"The Peppermint Snake Strangers," his friends responded at once!

"Who are the Peppermint Snake Strangers?" asked Sniggles.

"That's who we are to be careful of and who to stay away from. The Peppermint Snake Stranger is any stranger, and I'm not allowed to talk to strangers," Modesty replied nervously.

"Neither are we," Sniggles and Whispers replied at once.

They all began yelling at Ding Dong to warn him of the Peppermint Snake Stranger.

Luckily, they got his attention before any danger.

"Shh," said Modesty. "You hear that noise?"

They all became quiet to listen as they walked.

"Sss...sss...sss," they heard.

"Sss sss sss! Hi Kidsss. Would you like some of our Deliciousss Candiesss?" said a soft voice.

Modesty and his friends huddled together for safety. They were terrified
at the sight of the dreadful eyes staring back at them.

They were scared but continued walking trying to ignore them. The Peppermint Snake Stranger
was losing interest when suddenly Ding Dong said, "We're not allowed to talk to strangers."

"Oh, I'm not a stranger. I want to be your friend, and eat you...oops, I meant eat candy with you."

Modesty notices his friends weakening at the sight of all the candy, and
realized he had to do something, even though he was scared.

Just then, he remembered what his parents taught him, and thought of a plan.

"If you are not a stranger," Modesty asked, "then what is the password?"

"Yeah, what's the password," his friends joined in and repeated.

The Peppermint Snake Stranger asked Modesty, "What do you mean passssword?"

Modesty said, "If you do not know the password, then you are a stranger
and we will not talk to you. We are leaving. Come on guys!"

The Peppermint Snake Stranger looked in disbelief, and then started to slither away.

With a big sigh of relief, Modesty and his friends continued toward the park.

After passing the Peppermint Snake Stranger, they came into a clear view of the park. They heard birds chirping and tweeting the closer they became and it filled them with joy and excitement.

There was a fountain nearby and Modesty noticed birds bathing and splashing their wings in the water. He felt sad as he wondered to himself if he would ever be able to fly.

Whispers noticed the expression on Modesty's face, and decided to try and cheer him up.

In his soft, whispery voice, Whispers said, "Modesty that was really brave of you to stand up to the Peppermint Snake Stranger. You were smart to use the password."

"We didn't know the password was that powerful and could run strangers away," said Ding Dong.

"Thanks guys," said Modesty.

All of the sudden they all smelled something delicious in the air.

"Mmm, what's that smell," asked Sniggles?

"Smells sweet," said Whispers.

"Almost like candy!" said Ding Dong.

They were delighted by the wonderful aroma in the air, and they became
more excited as they reached the entrance to the park. When they
entered the park, it dawned on them of what they smelled.

Smiles broke out on their faces as they all exclaimed at once, " Mmm! Mmm! Bubble Gum!"

The scent of bubble gum was everywhere in the park.

They were taking in the sights, and as they neared some tables they became amazed as they realized who was sitting at one of the tables playing someone in a game of checkers.

They were so fascinated that they could not move. All they could do was smile, for right in front of them sat the great Bubble Gum Bunny.

Ding Dong recognized the girl playing Bubble Gum Bunny.

"That's Lee Lee the Lightening Bug playing Bubble Gum Bunny," said Ding Dong.

"She is my friend."

A million ideas and questions came to mind for Modesty as he stood and watched. As the game was coming to an end, Modesty wondered if he would get a chance to play Bubble Gum.

Lee Lee the Lightening Bug glanced to the side and noticed
Ding Dong as they drew closer to the table.

"Hi, Ding Dong," said Lee Lee, "What brings you here?"

"I came down with my friends to prepare for the big checker tournament," Ding Dong replied."

Ding Dong introduces everyone to Lee Lee.

"Nice to meet you," she said. "This is my friend, the great Bubble Gum Bunny!"

"Oh, we know," they all said together.

"Hi guys," said Bubble Gum Bunny

"If you are a butterfly,", "then where are your wings? Bubble Gum Bunny said to Modesty"

Modesty looked around sheepishly. "I have not developed my wings yet because I do not know how to live up to my name. My Papa said I should come here to ask if you could prepare me for the checker tournament and also maybe some pointers on how to earn my wings."

"Who is your Papa?" asked Bubble Gum Bunny.

"Unity Butterfly," said Modesty.

"Of Course!" exclaimed Bubble Gum Bunny. "Why didn't you say so?"

As the game ended, Bubble Gum Bunny, who won of course, displayed good sportsmanship to Lee Lee.

"Thank you for a fun game," he said, "would you like some bubble gum?"

Then Bubble Gum Bunny offered everyone some bubble gum.

"Thank you," they all responded.

As they all chewed bubble gum, and blew big bubbles, Bubble Gum
Bunny asked Modesty to join him in a game of checkers.

Modesty was filled with excitement as he approached the
table. His friends gathered around as he set up

the board, watching and looking on, as their little jaws chewed their gum.

"You all want to hear some stories," asked Bubble Gum Bunny.

"Yes," they responded.

"Good," said Bubble Gum Bunny. "Modesty, I want you to pay special attention to the stories I tell.

Bubble Gum Bunny began to tell all different kinds of stories. Some were funny and some
were serious. But all had a significant message. One particular story stuck out to Modesty as
he kept thinking about it, it was almost like a riddle. Modesty thought of the words again.

"You don't lose when you lose. You lose when you quit, and sometimes when
you lose you really win." Modesty thought and thought on these words.

He couldn't wait for the tournament.

The Big Day of The Checker Tournament.

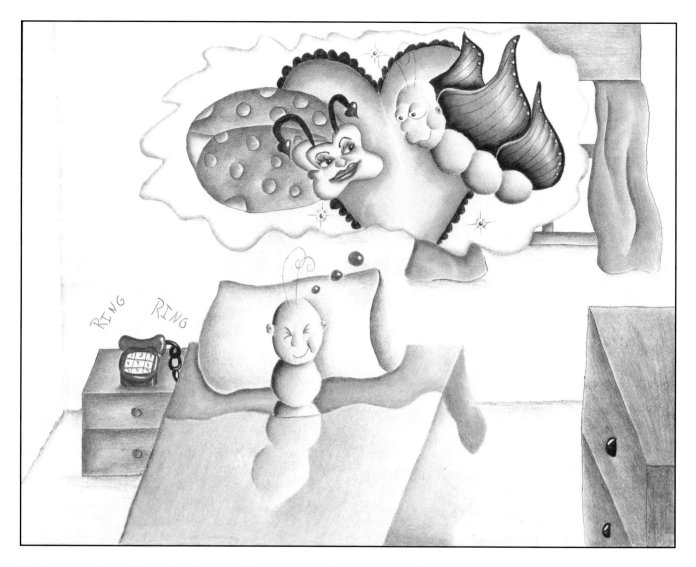

On the morning of the Big Checker Tournament, Modesty was fast asleep. He was in a very vivid dream.

He was happy in his dream because he was flying, and he had wings. He flew with confidence. He even approached Lisa the Lady Bug, who he had always had a crush on, but was too shy to even look her way.

As he approached her, the sky was filled with sparkles.

Suddenly, there was a loud ring, but he kept concentrating. Another loud ring, and he started to stir. By the third ring, Modesty slowly became awake and realized the house phone was ringing, and that he had been dreaming.

With reluctance, he got up to answer the phone.

In a sleepy voice, Modesty answered the phone, "Hello?"

"Good morning," said Ding Dong.

Recognizing the voice, Modesty said, "Good morning to you too, Ding Dong."

"I just wanted to be the first to wish you good luck in the checker tournament today," said Ding Dong.

"Oh, thank you," said Modesty. "I just had the most amazing dream."

"Tell me about it," said Ding Dong.

Modesty began telling Ding Dong about his dream, leaving nothing out. As their conversation continued, Modesty heard a beep, signaling that he had another call coming in.

"Hold on," he said to Ding Dong, "I have another call."

Modesty answers the other call to find his friend Whispers the Turtle on the line.

"Good morning, Whispers," said Modesty.

"Good morning, Modesty," Whispers replied

"I have Ding Dong on the other line. Do you mind if we all talk together?"

"Sure," said Whispers.

"Hey, Whispers," said Ding Dong.

"Hey, Ding Dong," said Whispers.

"So, what's going on Whispers," asked Modesty.

"Not much," he responded, "I'm at the store with Snigglze . He's in the mirror trying on hats to see which one to wear to the checker tournament today". "You know will be cheering for you!"

"Thanks," said Modesty. "I really appreciate all the support. I was just telling Ding Dong about a dream I had. Bubble Gum really got me thinking with the stories he told. They really inspired me."

"He's really smart," said Whispers.

"Yeah, and his stories are like riddles," said Ding Dong.

"But I think I understand his message," Modesty said proudly, "and I will show you today. I will try to apply it. said Modesty "Well, I'm about to get out of bed so I can get ready. I'll see you guys at the tournament. Thanks again for the support."

"See you there," said Whispers.

"Good luck," said Ding Dong as they all hung up.

Modesty ran into his father in the hallway.

"Good morning, Papa!" said Modesty.

"Hi son," Papa Unity said.

"It's not morning anymore, its afternoon now." "I didn't know it was
that late I was on the phone with my friends." said Modesty

"It's your big day, son," said Papa Unity. "It's good you got plenty of
rest. It will help you think better." Modesty smiled real big.

"Your mother and sister already left. She left your breakfast in the oven. Brush your
teeth, wash your face, and once you are finish eating, I will fly you to the tournament.

"Thanks Papa," said Modesty as he headed toward the bathroom wearing a huge confident smile.

After a nice hot shower, Modesty stood at the sink brushing his teeth. While looking in the mirror, he began to reflect on the words of the Great Bubble Gum Bunny.

He was filled with inspiration and motivation. He could already feel his wings begin to grow.

He knew he had a ways to go before he grew wings, but somehow he felt that was okay because he was on the right track. He left the bathroom and went to the kitchen.

Within minutes, Modesty was done eating his breakfast.

"Ready to go?" asked Unity.

"Ready as I'll ever be," said Modesty.

They headed out for the park!

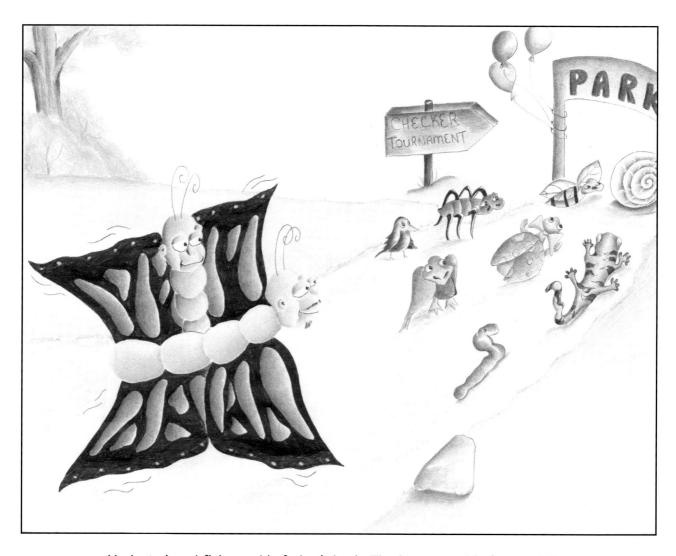

Modesty loved flying on his father's back. The breeze on his face and the
sight of his father's wings seemed to blow waves in the air.

As they were approaching the park, Papa asked, "Did you learn anything from Bubble Gum Bunny yesterday?

"Oh yes," said Modesty. "He told all kinds of stories that seemed like riddles, and they all had secret meanings."

"I knew you would learn something," said Papa Unity. "I'm glad you enjoyed meeting him."

They continued talking as they flew to the park.

They began to notice crowds of others headed toward the entrance of the
park, and the excitement began to build, as they entered the park.

After they landed they followed the crowd into the Park.

They noticed Marco the Mouse at a podium with a sign directing
people where to sign up for the checker tournament.

In the midst of all the excitement, Modesty noticed Lisa the Lady Bug coming directly toward him.

He immediately became nervous and shy, but it was too late to get shy.

"Hi, Modesty" she said softly. "Are you going to sign up for the checker tournament?"

"Ye-ye-yes," he stuttered. "I see it's a long line."

"Good luck and I'll be cheering for you!" Lisa the Lady Bug said with a smile.

Modesty responded more confidently, "Thank you, Lisa."

After they landed they followed the crowd into the Park.

They noticed Marco the Mouse at a podium with a sign directing
people where to sign up for the checker tournament.

In the midst of all the excitement, Modesty noticed Lisa the Lady Bug coming directly toward him.

He immediately became nervous and shy, but it was too late to get shy.

"Hi, Modesty" she said softly. "Are you going to sign up for the checker tournament?"

"Ye-ye-yes," he stuttered. "I see it's a long line."

"Good luck and I'll be cheering for you!" Lisa the Lady Bug said with a smile.

Modesty responded more confidently, "Thank you, Lisa."

Modesty took his number and went to his assigned place. He had chosen number 4. To gain confi dence, he searched the crowd for his family and friends.

He smiled when he saw them, and was happy for all their support.

Suddenly, Marco the Mouse came over the loud speaker in a squeaky voice, "Hear Ye, Hear Ye. I want to thank everyone for coming out to the 13th Annual Summer Fair Checker Tournament.

Will all the contestants please take your spots at the number you were assigned to?"

"The rules are very simple," Marco continued. "You must win two out of three games to move to the next round. If you lose twice, you are eliminated from the tournament. If you cheat you will be eliminated as well."

Marco continued explaining the prizes. "The winner will receive the 13th Annual

Summer Fair Checker Tournament Trophy and a Surprise Gift!"

"I wish you all good luck, but most importantly, have fun."

"Let the Games Begin!"

"My name is Modesty," he said with pride, as he introduced himself
to his opponent to get more acquainted with him.

"Hi, I'm Pickles the Beaver," responded Pickles in a goofy voice.

"Well nice to meet you, Pickles," said Modesty. "Good luck!"

They began the game, and as it progressed, Modesty was favored to win the first game of the best two out of three. Pickles had lots of fun, and Modesty displayed good sportsmanship.

As the game ended, Modesty said, "Good game," to Pickles.

"Thanks, Modesty," Pickles responded, "You are really good. You must practice a lot huh?"

Modesty humbly responded, "I try my hardest to do my very best, and I do not worry about failure."

As Modesty and Pickles started their second game of the tournament, they both heard a loud and arrogant, "Cockle-Doodle-Dooooo!!!"

It was the Red Tail Rooster who was favored to win the whole tournament.

Every time he made a good move or won a game, he would strut around arrogantly and tease his opponent. And at the top of his lungs he would scream, "Cockle-Doodle-Dooooo!"

It intimidated his opponent and the crowd burst with great applause feeding his ego.

Modesty stayed focused on the game. He was respectful of Pickles. He listened to Pickles, in his goofy and cheerful voice, explained how much he enjoyed eating all types of flavored pickles. Pickles hoped that the surprise gift was a whole box of pickles.

They both smiled as the game went on.

As the second game came to an end, Modesty eliminated Pickles. It was a fun game for both of them. Modesty could hear the cheers from his family and friends.

They both laughed and said their good-byes. Pickles wished Modesty good luck in the tournament

Several games were ending. Some lost. Some won. Everyone heard a very loud scream, "Cockle-Doodle-Dooooo!"

Lil Modesty noticed Sanchez the Salamander crying and terribly sad.

Modesty couldn't help but feel concerned for him.

"Hey Salamander," said Modesty, "What's wrong?"

In a whining tone Sanchez the Salamander spoke said, "I didn't win. I lost! I lost!"

As he continued crying he said, "The rooster is always teasing me. He said I was a loser!"

Modesty did not agree with the boasting, bragging, and teasing by Red Tail Rooster.

The rooster's behavior was affecting everyone.

Modesty took it upon himself to brighten up Sanchez the Salamander.

"You shouldn't cry," said Modesty.

Still sad, Sanchez the Salamander said, "but he keeps teasing me."

"Don't worry about anyone teasing you," said Modesty. "Words do not make you who you are, your actions do."

As the Salamander understood Modesty's meaning, he eventually stopped crying and became excited and began to smile again. Modesty continued to encourage Sanchez saying, "We are better and greater than a bunch of mean and bad words."

Sanchez the Salamander was thankful that Modesty came along and turned his frown upside down.

As they introduced themselves the Salamander told Modesty his name is Sanchez, and that he was from Mexico. Although he spoke a little English, he understood it more, than he could speak it.

With a warm embrace from Sanchez the Salamander, he wished Modesty good luck as he advanced toward the finals.

The tournament became more and more exciting. There were only six players left, and Lil Modesty was one of them. He kept his focus and even felt more confident than usual.

He even noticed Lisa the Lady Bug cheering him on.

The Red Tail Rooster continued his "Cockle-Doodle-Doooo," the whole time as he beat everyone that sat across from him. As he advanced to the finals the tournament became more intense.

The Chrissy the Chick and Crabby the Crab were both eliminated for cheating.

Now it was down to Modesty and Froggy the Frog. Whoever won would advance to the finals, and play the Red Tail Rooster.

It was close, but Modesty pulled it off, and was now headed for the finals!

Modesty displayed an enormous amount of sportsmanship to Froggy. They both had fun and really enjoyed themselves.

Froggy wished Modesty good luck as he entered the finals of the Big Checker Tournament.

"The finals are here! The finals are here!" exclaimed Marco in his high squeaky voice.

"The crowd cheered and clapped for the final two checker players, Lil Modesty and the Red Tail Rooster.

The air was filled with excitement.

Modesty's family and friends were so happy and proud that he made it to the finals.

The Red Tail Rooster continued screaming at the top of his lungs, "Cockle-Doodle-Doooo,".

Modesty tried introducing himself to the rooster, but he was too busy putting on for the crowd, screaming with such arrogance, boasting Cockle-Doodle-Doo's and flapping his wings, and strutting. Modesty stayed humble as Marco yelled to the crowd.

"Let the games begin!"

The tournament was heating up. The Red Tailed Rooster was extremely intimidating as he was screaming and opened his healthy colorful wings and tail, blocking the sun, Modesty could barely see the checker board.

Lil Modesty stayed humble and tried his best not to show fear, but he was nervous, and scared to play the Red Tail Rooster.

Unfortunately, Modesty lost the first game. He showed good sportsmanship as he said, "good game," but the Red Tail Rooster was too busy boasting to accept any sportsmanship from anyone.

Then he started to tease Modesty.

Modesty won the second game. It was now down to the final game. This would be the tiebreaker that will decide the winner of the Big Checker Tournament

Red Tail Rooster was really putting on a show. Cockle-Doodle-Doooo-ing while playing and covering most of the checker board with his healthy wings. The rooster was making all the right moves which put him in the lead.

Modesty became annoyed, and tried to remain calm, but was still irritated from all the yelling and teasing.

Suddenly, Modesty remembered what Bubble Gum Bunny told him about having a chance to demonstrate a form of modesty. Also, he remembered the riddle that stuck with him.

"You don't lose when you lose. You lose when you quit, and sometimes when you lose you really win."

Before Modesty knew it, the game was over. Red Tail Rooster won the game!

Red Tail was on fire with a ball of excitement.

He screamed proudly showing no sportsmanship at all.

Marco the Mouse yelled through the crowd with excitement, "Give a round of applause for our two finalists. They played so well."

The crowd went wild. The applause was to both finalist, but the Red Tail Rooster overshadowed Lil Modesty. He never had a chance to come to the front of the stage to receive the crowd's appreciation.

Red Tail was arrogantly showing off with no thought of sportsmanship toward Lil Modesty.

It did not bother Modesty that he did not win because he knew he played his best and tried hard.

He humbly stayed in the back while the Red Tail Rooster strutted cocky back and forth on the stage.

Marco spoke to Red Tail as he presented his trophy. "Here you are Red Tail Rooster, the trophy for the 13th Annual Summer Fair Checker Tournament. Also, here is your surprise gift!"

Red Tail released a loud, "Cockle-Doodle-Doooo!"

tail received the trophy without even a thank you to Marco the Mouse.

He then raced over anxiously to open the surprise gift. Everyone
held their breath in anticipation as he opened the gift.

Red Tail thought to himself, "maybe it is a great big bundle of bananas or maybe some gold. Or
maybe even chocolate covered corn on the cob. Oh boy!". Red Tails mind was racing everywhere.
He could not wait to brag about his special surprise gift, and tease everyone who did not win.

He finally opened the box and pulled out a shiny mirror. It was not a normal
mirror. This mirror shows the reflection of the true you. If you are beautiful
on the outside, but ugly inside, the refection will diminish your beauty.

When Red Tail looked in the mirror, everyone gasped in shock. The mirror had diminished Red
Tail's beautiful wings. Red Tail knew he was being ugly on the inside to his opponents.

He was in tears. He could not believe it.

Red Tail had been mean to everyone. He was screaming, bragging, boasting, and strutting around during the games.

Now he could not stand to look in the mirror and see his inner self. He dropped the mirror and as he covered his face and began to cry. As he was losing his feathers, he also knew he lost his chance to show any humbleness, modesty, or sportsmanship.

Everyone was still in shock at Red Tail's true appearance.

Lil Modesty then went towards the mirror, and looked down at his reflection and the most beautiful and amazing thing happened. His reflection smiled back at him, and as he stared, he felt a tickle on his back.

Marco the Mouse pointed at Lil Modesty and yelled, "Look, look!"

Modesty had sprouted the brightest, the most precious, the most colorful and the most adorable wings anyone had ever laid eyes on.

Modesty was so amazed and excited by what he was feeling. He immediately tried out his wings, and flew up to the sky.

His wings were not big,but adorably small. He understood for his wings to grow and develop, he had to gain more knowledge and wisdom on his journey through life.

Love was in the air as he felt he was living a dream, Lisa the Lady Bug made the moment more magical, when she flew up to the sky to congratulate him on his beautiful wings. As soon as they lay eyes on each other they both heard music in their little hearts.

Modesty thought to himself, "It's really fun to be modest."

Bubble-Gum-Bunny Safety-Tips!

1. Always have a family Secret Password.

2. Role-Play with your child to prepare them for any situation.

3. Never talk or accept anything from strangers.

4. Always have a "Safe House" in place for your child, in case of emergency.

Bubble Gum Bunny, Says:

Let's teach the little children about safety 1st.

(REPEAT 4X)

To practice and rehearse!

Let's teach the little children about safety first!

Safety First!

I.........................t's Safety First!

HEY LITTLE MODESTY,
WONDERING WHY HE HAS NO WINGS
ONE DAY YOU'LL REACH YOUR DREAMS,
AND YOUR GUNNA FLY, OH FLY
JUST GUNNA FLY, OH FLY

HEY LITTLE MODESTY,
WONDERIN WHY HE HAS NO WINGS,
GAINED TRUTH AND KNOWLEDGE DREAMS
AND YOU'RE GUNNA FLY, OH FLY,
JUST GUNNA FLY, OH FLY

HEY LITTLE MODESTY, WONDERIN WHY HE HAS NO WINGS
ONE DAY YOU'LL REACH YOUR DREAMS,AND YOUR GUNNA FLY, OH FLY
JUST GUNNA FLY, OH FLY

HERE HEY LITTLE MODESTY,
WONDERIN WHY HE HAS NO WINGS, GAINED TRUTH AND KNOWLEDGE DREAMS,
AND YOU'RE GUNNA FLY, OH FLY
JUST WANNA FLY, OH FLY
JUST GUUNA FLY, FLY, AWAY
JUST GUNNA FLY, FLY AWAY